Charlotte Turner Smith

Elegiac Sonnets

Charlotte Turner Smith

Elegiac Sonnets

ISBN/EAN: 9783337398064

Printed in Europe, USA, Canada, Australia, Japan

Cover: Foto ©Andreas Hilbeck / pixelio.de

More available books at **www.hansebooks.com**

BY

CHARLOTTE SMITH.

THE FIFTH EDITION,

WITH ADDITIONAL SONNETS

AND OTHER POEMS.

LONDON:

PRINTED FOR T. CADELL, IN THE STRAND,

M.DCC.LXXXIX.

TO

WILLIAM HAYLEY, Esq.

S I R,

WHILE I afk your protection for thefe
Effays, I cannot deny having myfelf fome efteem
for them. Yet permit me to fay, that did I not
truft to your candour and fenfibility, and hope
they will plead for the errors your judgment muft
difcover, I fhould never have availed myfelf of
the liberty I have obtained——that of dedicating
thefe fimple effufions to the greateft modern Mafter
of that charming talent, in which I can never be
more than a diftant copyift.

I am,

S I R,

Your moft obedient and obliged fervant,

CHARLOTTE SMITH.

PREFACE

FIRST AND SECOND EDITIONS.

─────────────

THE little Poems which are here called Sonnets, have I believe no very just claim to that title: but they consist of fourteen lines, and appear to me no improper vehicle for a single Sentiment. I am told, and I read it as the opinion of very good judges, that the legitimate Sonnet is ill calculated for our language. The specimen Mr. Hayley has given, though they form a strong exception, prove no more, than that the difficulties of the attempt vanish before uncommon powers.

Some very melancholy moments have been beguiled, by expressing in verse the sensations those moments brought.

brought. Some of my friends, with partial indiscretion, have multiplied the copies they procured of several of these attempts, till they found their way into the prints of the day in a mutilated state; which concurring with other circumstances, determined me to put them into their present form. I can hope for readers only among the few, who to sensibility of heart, join simplicity of taste.

PREFACE

TO THE

THIRD AND FOURTH EDITIONS.

THE reception given by the public, as well as my particular friends, to the two first Editions of these Poems, has induced me to add to the present such other Sonnets as I have written since, or have recovered from my acquaintance, to whom I had given them without thinking well enough of them at the time to preserve any copies myself. A few of those last written, I have attempted on the Italian model; with what success I know not, but I am persuaded that to the generality of readers those which are less regular will be more pleasing.

As

As a few notes were neceſſary, I have added them at the end. I have there quoted ſuch lines as I have borrowed; and even where I am conſcious the ideas were not my own, I have reſtored them to their original poſſeſſors.

PREFACE.

TO THE

FIFTH EDITION.

———————

IN printing a list of so many noble, literary, and respectable names, it would become me, perhaps, to make my acknowledgments to those friends, to whose exertions in my favor, rather than to any merit of my own, I owe the brilliant assemblage. With difficulty I repress what I feel on this subject; but in the conviction that such acknowledgments would be painful to them, I forbear publicly to speak of those particular obligations, the sense of which will ever be deeply impressed on my heart.

SUB-

SUBSCRIBERS.

N. B. The figures fignify the number of copies fubfcribed for.

Her Royal Highnefs the Duchefs of Cumberland, 10 copies

A

Dowager Countefs of Albemarle
Earl of Ailfbury, 2
Countefs of Abingdon
Earl of Abergavenny, 5
Countefs of Abergavenny, 5
Countefs of Antrim
Lord Apfley, 2
Lady Jane Afton, 2
Sir Willoughby Afton, Bart. 2
Sir Thomas Acland, Bart.
Lady Acland
Rt. Hon. Sir R. P Arden
Lady Arden
Henry Addington, Efq. 2
John Hiley Addington, Efq. 6
Mifs Addington, 2

W. A. Acourt, Efq.
George Arnold Arnold, Efq. 2
William Aiderfley, Efq.
John Julius Angerftein, Efq. 2
Rev. Charles Afhburnham
Rev. William Alcock
Rev. Charles Alcock
Rev. Robert Afhe
Mrs. Allen
Mrs. Aufrere
Mifs Catharine Afhburnham
Mifs Afhley
Mifs Akerman
Mifs Altham
Mrs. Amyatt
Dr. Afh, F. R. S.

B

The Duchefs of Beaufort
The Duke of Buccleugh
The Duchefs of Buccleugh
Lord Bulkeley
Lady Bulkeley
Lord Bruce
Lord Bofton
Lady Bofton
Lady Lucy Doyle

Hon. Mrs. Bofcawen
Hon. Mrs. Bouverie
Hon. Mrs. Bailey
Hon. Mrs. E. Bouverie
Hon. Mifs Browne
Rt. Hon. Lieut. Gen. Burgoyne.
Lady B. Bouverie
Hon. B. Bouverie
Dowager Lady Beaumont, 2

b

Sir George Beaumont, Bart. 2
Lady Beaumont, 4
Lady Brooke
Hon. Mrs. Broderic
Colonel Baily
Mifs Baily
General Bruce
Mifs Brooke
Charles Bragge, Efq.
William Bragge, Efq.
William Bray, Efq.
C. Broughton, Efq.
George Biggin, Efq.
William Becket, Efq.
Barrington Bradfhaw, Efq.
Redmond Barry, Efq.
William Bifhop, Efq. 2
Mrs. Bragge
Mrs. Beckford
Mrs. Bifhop, 2
John Bifhop, Efq. 2
Mrs. J. Bifhop, 2
John Brathwaite, Efq. 2
Francis Baffet, Efq.
Stukely Buck, Efq.
Francis Barroneau, Efq.
Jacob Bryant, Efq. 2
John Bowdler, Efq.
Richard Bettefworth, Efq.
William Branfton, Efq.
Rev. Charles Blackftone
Rev. Mr. Baker
Rev. Mr. Brooke
Rev. Mr. Berwick
Rev. Dr. Bathurft
Mrs. Browne
Mrs. Boehm
Mrs. Bohan
Mrs. Bowdler
Mrs. Buckner
Mrs. Benyon

Mrs. Bramfton
Mrs. Brocas
Mrs. Bowles, 2
Mrs. Burton
Mrs. Blair
Mrs. Bifcoe
Mrs. Bowdler, Bath, 2
Mrs. Augufta Bloodworth
Richard Barwell, Efq. 2
Mrs. Barwell, 4
Mifs Bowdler
Mifs Harriet Bowdler, 2
Mifs Berens, 2
Mifs Berens
Mifs Catharine Berens
Mifs Burney
Mr. Hawkins Browne, 2
Mr. Alexander Blair
Mr. Bufhby
Mr. Bennet
Edmund Boehm, Efq. 2
Mrs. E. Boehm
Mifs Berney
Mrs. Biddulph
Mrs. Barry
Mifs Benfon
Mr. Baker
Mrs. Boiffiere
James Buller, Efq,
The Briftol Library Society
Mrs. Blackman
Mrs. Brancas
William Bromfield, Efq.
Samuel Bevor, Efq.
Mifs Briftow
Mifs D. Blackwood
Mifs Blackman
Mifs F. Blackman
Mifs Bayley
J. T. Batt, Efq.
Henry Beaufoy, Efq. 2

Rev. Dr. Barford
Dr. Baily
Dr. Beauvoir, 2
Mrs. Beauvoir, 2
Mr. Beckett
Mr. R. Baker
The late John Berridge, Esq. 2

Mrs. Beaufoy, 2
Francis Burton, Esq.
Alexander Brodie, Esq. 5
Matthew Bunbury, Esq.
John Blackburn, Esq.
Mrs. Blackburn

C.

The Duke of Chandos, 20
The Duchess of Chandos, 20
The Archbishop of Canterbury, 2
Dowager Countess of Clanricarde, 6
Earl of Clanricarde, 5
Countess of Clanricarde, 5
Earl of Corke, 2
Countess of Corke
Earl of Cavan
Countess of Cavan
Countess of Charlemont
Lord Viscount Cremorne,
Lady Viscountess Cremorne, 2
Lord Frederic Campbell
Lady Frederic Campbell
Lady Louisa Conolly, 2
Lady Mary Coke
Lady Foster Cunliffe
Sir Edward Crofton, Bart.
Lady Crofton, 2
Lady Cottrell, 2
Rt. Hon. Thomas Conolly, 2
Sir John Coghill, Bart.
Rev. Mr. Crowe
Mr. J. Caldecot
Mrs. Chambers
Mrs. Corry
Mrs. Clements
Mr. Croker, 2
Mrs. Croker
Mr. Conrad

Mr. William Curties
Miss Cranmer
Mrs. Carter
Miss E. Carter
John Walbank Childers, Esq.
John Crowder, Esq.
Michael Colling, Esq. 2
William Chesson, Esq.
John Chichester, Esq.
Charles Coles, Esq.
—— Cordwell, Esq.
Richard Cox, Esq.
Rev. Mr. Carwardine
Rev. Robert Cranmer
Pole Carew, Esq.
Isaac Corry, Esq. 2
William Morgan Clyfford, Esq.
Mr. Richard Corbould
Mrs. Childers
Miss Mary Cater
Geo. James Chomondeley, Esq.
William Chamberlayne, Esq. 2
Miss Chamberlayne
Miss C. Chamberlayne
John Call, Esq. 2
Mrs. Call, 2
Miss Call, 2
J. F. Cawthorne, Esq. 2
Mrs. Cawthorne
Miss Cousmaker
Mrs. Coate

Mrs. Cholmley, 2

Mrs. Philadelphia Cogan

Mrs. Frances Chambers

Mrs. Peter Cazalet

Mrs. Clarke

Henry Crockatt, Efq.

J. Godfalve Croffe, Efq.

Mrs. Croftc

D.

Earl of Darlington

Countefs of Darlington

The Countefs of Derby, 2

Lady Amelia De Burgh, 2

Lady Augufta Dillon, 2

Lady Frances Douglas, 2

Hon. John Thomas De Burgh, 2

Sir John Dick, Bart. 2

Luke Dillon, Efq. 2

Mr. Deane, 6

Mr. Court D'Ewes

Mrs. Dance, 2

George Dance, Efq.

Mr. Dobfon

Mrs. Dodfworth

Mrs. Arthur Dawfon, 2

Mifs Araminta Dawfon

Mrs. Drake, 2

Mifs F. Dowker

Mifs Davenport

Mrs. Delany

Mrs. D'Oyley

Mrs. Dixon

Jeremiah Dyfon, Efq.

Mrs. Dyfon

Mifs E. Dyfon

Mifs F. Dyfon

George Dyfon, Efq.

Rev. Mr. Dampier

Rev. Mr. Dodd

Mrs. Richard Dawfon

Mifs Duer, 2

Mifs Frances Duer, 2

Mifs Elizabeth Duer, 2

Rev. Rowland Duer, 2

Mrs. Duer, 2

Mifs Duer, 2

Mifs D'Aguilar

Alexander Davifon, Efq. 2

Archibald Douglas, Efq 2

Nathaniel Dance, Efq.

Mrs. Dance

Lionell Darell, Efq.

Mrs. Darell

C. Davy, M. B.

John Dawes, Efq.

Mrs. Dawes

Mifs Duncombe

E.

The Earl of Effingham, 2

Sir Harry Englefield, Bart. 2

The Dean of Ely

The Provoft of Eton

Mrs. Ettwick

Mifs Ellis

Mifs Ewer

William Benfon Earle, Efq.

Hon. E. J. Elliot, 2

John Thomas Ellis, Efq.

Mrs. Ellis

F.

Lord Fairford
Lady Fairford
Lord Henry Fitzgerald
Hon. Mifs Fox
Sir John Frederic, Bart.
Lady Frederic
Mrs. Fitzgerald
Mrs. Fermor
Mrs. Henry Fermor
Mrs. Fielde
Mrs. M. Ford

Mrs. G. Farhill
Mifs Fauquier
Mifs Fanfhawe
John Fanfhawe, Efq.
Rev. Edmund Ferrers
Mrs. Ferrers
John Fuller, Efq. 2
John Fuller, Efq. 2
J. Frere, Efq.
Rev. J. T. Fearon

G.

The Duke of Gordon
The Duchefs of Gordon
The Marquis of Graham, 2
The Earl of Guildford
Rt. Hon. Mr. Grenville
Hon. Mrs. Gage
Hon. Mrs. Levefon Gower
Hon. Mr. Juftice Gould
Lady Gould
Hon. Mr. Juftice Grofe
Lady Grofe
Sir Sampfon Gideon, Bart. 2
Mrs. Gage
Rev. Dr. Griffin
Rev. Dr. Glaffe
Rev. Mr. Gould
Rev. Dr. Gordon
Ambrofe Goddard, Efq. 2
Mrs. Goddard, 2
Mifs Goddard
William Grove, Efq. 2

Rev. Mr. Glaffe
Rev. William Stanley Goddard
Mrs. Goodenough, 2
Mrs. Goddard, 2
Rev. Mr. Gay
Mrs. Gould
Mrs. Gunning
Mrs. Godfchall
Mifs Grove
John Grant, Efq. 2
Robert Gordon, Efq.
Thomas Gould, Efq.
Thomas Griffin, Efq.
George Griffin, Efq.
Richard Gray, Efq. 2
T. Green, Efq.
Dr. Glynn
Mr. Galliard, 2
Mr. William Guy
Mifs Godfalve
Mr. H. Gardner, 50

H.

The Marquis of Huntly
Lord Hood

Late Hon. Mrs. Hoare
Sir Alexander Hood, K. B

Sir Andrew Hammond, Bart.
Lady Hammond
Late Sir Richard Hoare, Bart. 2
Lady Hoare, 2
Sir Richard Colt Hoare, Bart. 2
Henry Hoare, Efq. 2
Henry Hugh Hoare, Efq. 2
Charles Hoare, Efq. 2
Lady Herries
Lady Hales, 2
Lady Hefketh
John James Hamilton, Efq.
William Hayley, Efq.
Mrs. Hayley
General Hervey, 2
Mrs. Hamilton
Sir William Hillman
Mrs. Hofkins, 2
Mrs. Hervey
Mrs. Hannay
Mrs. Holbeck
Gilbert Heathcot, Efq.
Mrs. Hill
Mrs. Hicks
Mrs. Holder

Mrs. Hay
Mrs. Heathcot
Mrs. Harcourt
Mr Holbeck
Rev. George J. Huntingford
Rev. Mr. Harrifon
Rev. Mr. Heath, Eton College
Harry Harmood, Efq. 2
James Holder, Efq.
Rev. Mr. Hare
Mifs Hodgefon
Mifs Sarah Hodgefon
Mrs. Hockley
Mifs Hanbury
Mifs F. Hanbury
Mr. Hill
Mrs. Heron
Mr. Hutchinfon
Thomas Hubbert, Efq. 2
John Henniker, Efq.
John Hunter, Efq.
Mr. T. Harrifon
Mrs. Handcock
Mr. Hughs
Jofiah Heathcot, Efq.

I. J.

Rt. Hon. Richard Jackfon
Lady Jarvis
Lady Impey, 2
Lady Jones
Jofeph Jekyl, Efq.
Robert Incledon, Efq.
Eyles Irwin, Efq.
Mrs. Irwin
George Jackfon, Efq.
Mrs. Jackfon
Mifs Ifham
Rev. Mr. Johns
Mrs. Johns

Mifs Ironmonger
Rev. ——— Iremonger
Mifs Iremonger
Mrs. Iremonger
A. E. Impey, Efq.
Morton James, Efq.
John Jones, Efq.
John Jorden, Efq.
Late John Jennings, Efq.
Hugh Inglis, Efq.
Mifs Jennings, 2
Mifs Mary Ingram

K.

Lord Kenyon
Lady Kenyon
Dr. Kydd
Dr. Kirkland

Richard Payne Knight, Efq.
Mr. Kynnerſley
Thomas Knight, Efq.

L.

The Duke of Leinſter
The Duchefs of Leinſter
Countefs Ligonier, 2
Lord Lovaine, 4
Lady Lovaine, 4
The Biſhop of London, 4
Lady Louiſa Lennox, 2
Hon. Mrs. Temple Luttrell
Late Hon. James Luttrell
Hon. Mr. Legge
Robert Lee, Efq.
Rev. Dr. Lee, Warden Win. Coll.
Mrs. Lee
Harry Lee, Efq.
Launcelot Lee, Efq.
Rev. George Law
Mr. Long
Captain Lafcelles, 2
William Lafcelles, Efq. 2
Mrs. Luther
Mr. Luſhington

Mrs. Luſhington
Thomas Le Meſurier, Efq.
Paul Le Meſurier, Efq.
Benjamin Lethuillier, Efq. 2
Dr. Littlehale
Mifs Hannah Lightbody
John Long, Efq.
Charles Lambert, Efq.
Captain Linzee
John Longley, Efq.
Mrs. Longley
Rev. Thomas Lear
———————— Locke, Efq. 4
Late W. M. Leaves, Efq.
Mr. Loyd
Mrs. Matilda Lockwood
John Lavie, Efq.
Mrs. Lee
Mrs. Lloyd
S. M. Leake, Efq.

M.

The Duke of Montague
The Earl of Mornington
Lord Mulgrave, 4
Lady Vifcountefs Montague
Lord Montmorres
Lord Maitland
Baron Metge, 6
Rt. Hon. Frederic Montague

Sir William Mufgrave, Bart
Hon. Mrs. Marſham
Sir Hector Monro, Bart.
Sir Alexander Monro
Sir Thomas Miller, Bart.
Lady Miller
Mrs. Montague, 3
Mifs Milner

Mifs M. Milner
Mifs L. Milner
Rev. H. Milner
Mrs. B. Matthew
Edward Morgan, Efq.
Mrs. Morgan
Late Jeremiah Meyer, Efq.
Alexander Mackenzie, Efq.
Mrs. Moore
Mrs. Marfton
Mifs M'Cleverty, 2
John Maddifon, Efq. 4
Mrs. Man
Mrs. Mee
Langford Millington, Efq.
Rev. Michael Marlow

Mr. Morrow
—— Mills, Efq.
Mrs. Marchant
Mrs. Mordaunt
Mrs. Mafter
Mrs. Moyfey
Mrs. Morgan
Mr. J. Mander
Colonel Mitchell
Mifs Middleton
William Mollefon, Efq.
William Mitford, Efq. 20
Matthew Montague, Efq. 2
Mrs. Montague, 2
Mifs Montrefor
Rev. Mr. Milton

N.

The Duchefs of Northumberland
Late Countefs of Northington, 2
Countefs of Newburgh
Earl of Newburgh
Lord North
Lady North
Hon. Colonel North, 2
Hon. Major North, 2
Hon. Frederick North
Hon. Mifs North
Sir Stafford Northcote, Bart.

Lady Sarah Napier
Hon. Mifs Neville
Lady Norcliffe
Richard Nafh, Efq.
Mifs Neville
Mrs. Newton
Rev. Mr. Newbolt, 2
Nicholas Nicholas, Efq.
T. P. Newhoufe, Efq.
Francis Newbery, Efq.

O.

Rt. Hon. John O'Niell, 10
Hon. Mrs. O'Niell, 10
Hon. John Luttrell Olmius, 2
Hon. Mrs. Olmius, 2
Mifs Olmius, 2
Lady Ogle

Mrs. Ogle
Mrs. Oliver
Paul Orchard, Efq.
—— Ord, Efq.
Mrs. Ord
Mifs Ord, 2

P.

Rt. Hon. William Pitt, 2
Lady Annabella Polwarth
Lord Palmerston, 2
Lady Palmerston, 2
Lady Caroline Peachy, 2
Sir James Peachy, Bart.
Hon. Mrs. Pitt, 2
Hon. Philip Pusey, 4
Hon. Henry Pelham
Miss Pulteney, 2
Mr. Pulteney, 2
Lady Hyde Parker
Mrs. Poulter
Miss Pyke
Miss C. Piers
Mrs. Parry Price
Mrs. Pigot
Miss Pym, 2
Rev. Walston Pym, 2
Rev. Charles Parsons
Anthony Parkin, Esq. 2

Mr. Peters
Thomas Phipps, Esq.
Miss Phipps
Miss Harriet Phipps
Miss Peckham
William Parsons, Esq.
Mrs. Pollhill
Norton Powlet, Esq.
Arthur Pigot, Esq.
Mrs. Pinsold
Rev. Mr. Preston
Miss Porter
John Peachy, Esq.
Miss Philips
Rev. Dr. Pennington
———— Price, Esq.
Mrs. Porteous, 2
Mrs. Peck, 2
James Poole, Esq.
Mrs. Maurice Pugh
Rev. Mr. Pitt, 2

Q.

Andrew Quick, Esq.

John Quick, Esq.

R.

Late Duke of Rutland, 10
Dutchess of Rutland
Dowager Countess of Radnor, 2
Lord Rivers, 2
Hon. Colonel Rodney
Hon. Mrs. Rodney
John Robinson, Esq. 5
Mrs. Robinson, 5
George Rose, Esq. 20
George Poyntz Ricketts, Esq.
John Richards, Esq. 4
George Romney, Esq.

Mrs. Ricketts
Mrs. Rawdon
John Rolle, Esq.
Mrs. Roberts
Rev. Mr. Roberts
Mr. Samuel Rogers
Mr. Ring
Rev. Mr. Richards, 2
Mrs. Ryder
John Rolle, Esq.
Mrs. Rolle
George Henry Rose, Esq.

Thomas Ridge, Efq.
Mrs. Ridge

Mrs. Rainsford

S.

Earl Stanhope
Countefs Stanhope
Dowager Countefs Spencer
Lady Vifcountefs Strangford
Lord Sandys
Lady Sandys
Lord St. Afaphs
Late Bihop of St. Afaphs
Hon. John St. John
Hon. Mrs. Sentleger
Hon. Captain Sentleger
Hon. Keith Stewart
Hon. Mrs. Keith Stewart
Sir Harry St. John, Bart.
Lady St. John
Sir John Sebright
Lady Sebright
Lady Stewart
Lady Shelly
Mifs Stewart
Mifs Maria Sentleger
The Dean of St. Afaphs
Mrs. Shipley, 2
Mifs Shipley, 2
Mifs C. L. Shipley
Mrs. W. Shipley
W. C. Sloper, Efq. 2
Mrs. Sloper
Mifs Sloper
Colonel Sherriffe, 2
Mrs. Sherriffe, 2
Mrs. L. Smith
Mrs. S. Smith
Jofias Smith, Efq.
Thomas Smith, Ffq.
Mrs. Charles Smith

William Smith, Efq.
Walter Smythe, Efq.
Mrs. Smythe
Rev. Dr Smyth
Mrs. Smyth
His Excellency John Strange
—— Seymour, Efq.
W. Sealy, Efq.
Rev. Mr. Spragge, 2
Mrs. Stratford
Mrs. Sutton, 6
Mrs. Sampfon
David Stevenfon, Efq.
Dr. Sanden
Mrs. Steele
—— Senior, Efq.
Captain Swinney
Henry Shelly, Efq.
Henry Shelly, Efq. jun.
George Shiffner, Efq.
Mrs. Siddons, 2
Mifs Slaney
Rev. Mr. Salmon
Dr. Skeete
Rev. Dr. Shepherd
William Seward, Efq.
Richard Vernon Sadlier, Efq.
William Sotheby, Efq.
John Steers, Efq.
Charles Steers, Efq.
Edward Steers, Efq.
James Steers, Efq.
Mifs Sheffield
Mr. S. Squire
Mr. Salmon
Mrs. Sharman

William Smith, Efq.
Mrs. Smith, Coopers Hall
Jofeph Smith, Efq.
Robert Smith, Efq.
Mrs. Smith
Mifs Stafford
Mr. George Smith
John Sargent, Jun. Efq. 6
Mrs. Sargent
Hans Sloane, Efq.
Mifs Sharman
Mrs. Streatfield
Thomas Steele, Efq.
R. T. Sullivan, Efq.

John Shakefpeare, Efq.
Mrs. Sullivan
Mrs. Shakefpeare
John Sargent, Efq. 2
Mrs. Sargent
Mifs Stephens
Mr. Seward
John Stanley, Efq.
Mrs. Stanley
George Sumner, Efq.
Mrs. Sumner
Mifs Some.ville
Mifs Louifa Somerville
Mifs St. Maure

T.

The Earl of Tyrconnel
The Countefs of Tyrconnel
The Archbifhop of Tuam, 2
Lady Bridget Tollemache
Dowager Lady Tichbourne
Sir Harry Tichbourne, Bart.
Lady Tichbourne
Lady Thomas
Sir John Trevelyan, Bart.
Charles Townfend, Efq.

William Davenport Talbot, Efq.
———— Tuffnell, Efq.
Mrs. Trevillian
Mifs Trevillian
Mrs. Trotman
Dominic Trant, Efq.
Mifs Tireman
John Townfon, Efq. 2
T. Towers, Efq.

U. V.

Lady Vernon
Mrs. Vefey
Rev. George Vanburgh
Mr. Udney

Robert Udney, Efq. 2
Mrs. Udney
Mifs Vernon

W.

The Earl of Warwick, 2
The Countefs of Warwick, 2
Lord Walfingham, 2
Lady Walfingham, 2
The Bifhop of Winchefter
Lady Williams
Hon. Horace Walpole

Rev. Dr. Warton
Rev. Thomes Warton
Mrs Wegg
Mifs Wegg
Mifs S. Wegg
Mr. G. Wegg
Mrs. Walter

HenryPenruddockWyndham,Efq.
Mrs. Walker
Dalhoufie Watherftone, Efq.
Mrs. Watherftone
Rev. T. Walker
Mifs Williams
———Weddell, Efq. 2
Mrs. Wathen
Mrs. Williams
Mr. Wool
Rev. Charles Webber
Mr. Weller, 2
Hill Willfon, Efq.
Mr. John Willing Warren

Mrs. Wroughton
Mrs. Williams
Rev. Dr. Warner
Rev. Mr. Wray
Mr. Woodhull
Mifs Willes
Mrs. Weddell
John Warburton, Efq.
W. Wilberforce, Efq.
John Wigglefworth, Efq.
John Wilmot, Efq.
Mrs. Wilmot
Mifs Wikes
Mifs Wrightfon

Y.

Mifs Yonge, 2

☞   The Refidences of Subfcribers are not inferted, unlefs in a few inftances where it appeared abfolutely neceffary; as fuch addition would have encreafed the fize of the lift too much.

SUBSCRIBERS NAMES,

omitted by mistake, or received too late for insertion in the list,

The Duke of Marlborough 2
The Duchess of Marlborough 2
Mrs. Adams
Mrs. Bradney
Mrs. Bradylle
William Cooper, Esq.
—— Coore, Esq.
Mrs. Coore
Mrs. Davison
Lady D'Oyley, 2
Samuel Gardiner, Esq.
Mrs. Gale
Dr. Hervey

Mrs. Lucas
Mrs. Lewis
Mrs. N. Lewis
William Lucas, Esq. 2
Mrs. Milton
Job Mathew, Esq.
Samuel Phipps, Esq.
Thomas Raikes, Esq.
Miss Rich
Mrs. Saunders
Mrs. Sutherland
William Steer, Esq.
Mrs. Townley

CONTENTS.

SONNETS.

		Page
I.	- - - - - - -	I
II.	Written at the clofe of Spring •	2
III.	To a Nightingale - - -	3
IV.	To the Moon - - - -	4
V.	To the South Downs - • -	5
VI.	To Hope - - - • -	6
VII.	On the Departure of the Nightingale	7
VIII.	To Spring - - - -	8
IX.	- - - - - - - -	9
X.	To Mrs. G. - - - - -	10
XI.	To Sleep - - - - -	11
XII.	Written on the Sea Shore - -	12
XIII.	From Petrarch - - - -	13

Page

XIV.   From the fame ·   ·   ·   14

XV.   ° From the fame ·   ·   ·   15

XVI.   From the fame ·   ·   ·   16

XVII.   From the Thirteenth Cantata of Metaftafio 17

XVIII.   To the Earl of Egremont -   18

XIX.   To Mr. Hayley -   -   -   19

XX.   To the Countefs of A—— -   20

XXI.   Suppofed to be written by Werter   21

XXII.   By the fame -   -   -   -   22

XXIII.   By the fame -   -   -   -   23

XXIV.   By the fame -   ·   -   -   24

XXV.   By the fame -   -   -   -   25

XXVI.   To the River Arun -   -   26

XXVII.   -   -   -   -   -   -   27

XXVIII. To Friendfhip -   -   -   28

XXIX.   To Mifs C—— ·   -   -   29

XXX.   To the River Arun -   -   30

Page

XXXI.   Written in Farm Wood, on the South
          Downs, May, 1784   -   -   31

XXXII.   To Melancholy.   Written on the
          Banks of the Arun   •   •   32

XXXIII.   To the Naiad of the Arun   -   33

XXXIV.   To a Friend   `   •   -   -   34

XXXV.   To Fortitude   -   •   •   •   35

XXXVI.   -   -   -   -   -   -   36

XXXVII.   Sent to the Honorable Mrs. O'Niell,
          with painted flowers   -   -   37

XXXVIII. From the Novel of Emmeline   38

XXXIX.   To Night.   From the fame   -   39

XL.   From the fame   -   -   -   40

XLI.   To Tranquillity   -   -   .   41

XLII.   Compofed during a walk on the Downs,
          in November, 1787   -   -   42

XLIII.   •   -   -   -   -   -   43

Page

XLIV.　Written in the church yard at Middleton in Suffex　-　-　-　44

XLV.　On leaving a part of Suffex　-　45

XLVI.　Written at Penfhurft, in Autumn, 1788　46

XLVII.　To Fancy　-　-　-　-　47

XLVIII.　To Mrs. * * * *　-　-　-　48

Ode to Defpair. From the novel of Emmeline　49

Elegy　-　-　-　-　-　-　52

Song. From the French of Cardinal Bernis　57

The Origin of Flattery　-　-　-　-　59

ELEGIAC

ELEGIAC SONNETS.

SONNET I.

THE partial Mufe, has from my earlieft hours
  Smil'd on the rugged path I'm doom'd to tread,
And ftill with fportive hand has fnatch'd wild flowers,
  To weave fantaftic garlands for my head:
But far, far happier is the lot of thofe
  Who never learn'd her dear delufive art;
Which, while it decks the head with many a rofe,
  Referves the thorn, to fefter in the heart.
For ftill fhe bids foft Pity's melting eye
  Stream o'er the ills fhe knows not to remove,
Points every pang, and deepens every figh
  Of mourning friendfhip, or unhappy love.
Ah! then, how dear the Mufe's favors coft,
  If thofe paint forrow beft—who feel it moft! 14

B   SONNET

SONNET II.

WRITTEN AT THE CLOSE OF SPRING.

THE garland's fade that Spring fo lately wove,
  Each fimple flower, which fhe had nurs'd in dew,
Anemonies, that fpangled every grove,   3
  The primrofe wan, and hare-bell, mildly blue.
No more fhall violets linger in the dell,
  Or purple orchis variegate the plain,
Till Spring again fhall call forth every bell,
  And drefs with humid hands her wreaths again.—
Ah! poor humanity! fo frail, fo fair,
  Are the fond vifions of thy early day,
Till tyrant paffion, and corrofive care,
  Bid all thy fairy colours fade away!
Another May new buds and flowers fhall bring;
Ah! why has happinefs——no fecond Spring?

SONNET

SONNET III.

TO A NIGHTINGALE.

POOR melancholy bird——that all night long   r
   Tell'ſt to the Moon thy tale of tender woe;
   From what ſad cauſe can ſuch ſweet ſorrow flow,
And whence this mournful melody of ſong?

Thy poet's muſing fancy would tranſlate
   What mean the ſounds that ſwell thy little breaſt,
   When ſtill at dewy eve thou leav'ſt thy neſt,
Thus to the liſtening night to ſing thy fate?

Pale Sorrow's victims wert thou once among,
   Tho' now releas'd in woodlands wild to rove?
   Say—haſt thou felt from friends ſome cruel wrong,
Or died'ſt thou——martyr of diſaſtrous love?
Ah! ſongſtreſs ſad! that ſuch my lot might be,
To ſigh and ſing at liberty——like thee!
            B 2   SONNET

SONNET IV.

TO THE MOON.

QUEEN of the filver bow!—by thy pale beam,
　Alone and penfive, I delight to ftray,
And watch thy fhadow trembling in the ftream,
　Or mark the floating clouds that crofs thy way.
And while I gaze, thy mild and placid light
　Sheds a foft calm upon my troubled breaft;
And oft I think,——fair planet of the night,
　That in thy orb, the wretched may have reft:
The fufferers of the earth perhaps may go,
　Releas'd by death——to thy benignant fphere,
And the fad children of defpair and woe
　Forget in thee, their cup of forrow here.
Oh! that I foon may reach thy world ferene,
Poor wearied pilgrim——in this toiling fcene!

SONNET

Plate 1   Sonnet 4

Publish'd Jan.ʳ 1 1789 by T.Cadell, Strand.

Queen of the Silver Bow, &c

SONNET V.

TO THE SOUTH DOWNS.

AH! hills belov'd!——where once, an happy child,

   Your beechen fhades, 'your turf, your flowers among,'2

I wove your blue-bells into garlands wild,

   And woke your echoes with my artlefs fong.

Ah! hills belov'd!——your turf, your flow'rs remain;

   But can they peace to this fad breaft reftore,

For one poor moment foothe the fenfe of pain,

   And teach a breaking heart to throb no more?

And you, Aruna!——in the vale below, 9

   As to the fea your limpid waves you bear,

Can you one kind Lethean cup beftow,

   To drink a long oblivion to my care?

Ah! no!——when all, e'en Hope's laft ray is gone,

There's no oblivion——but in death alone!

SONNET VI.

TO HOPE.

OH, Hope! thou foother fweet of human woes!
  How fhall I lure thee to my haunts forlorn!
For me wilt thou renew the wither'd rofe,
  And clear my painful path of pointed thorn?
Ah come, fweet nymph! in fmiles and foftnefs dreft,
  Like the young hours that lead the tender year,
Enchantrefs come! and charm my cares to reft:——
  Alas! the flatterer flies, and will not hear!
A prey to fear, anxiety, and pain,
  Muft I a fad exiftence ftill deplore;
Lo!——the flowers fade, but all the thorns remain,
  ' For me the vernal garland blooms no more.' 12
Come then ' pale Mifery's love!' be thou my cure 13
And I will blefs thee, who tho' flow art fure.

SONNET

SONNET VII.

ON THE DEPARTURE OF THE NIGHTINGALE.

SWEET poet of the woods——a long adieu! .
   Farewel, soft minstrel of the early year!
Ah! 'twill be long ere thou shalt sing anew,
   And pour thy music on the ' night's dull ear.' 4
Whether on Spring thy wandering flights await, 5
   Or whether silent in our groves you dwell,
The pensive muse shall own thee for her mate, 7
   And still protect the song, she loves so well.
With cautious step, the love-lorn youth shall glide
   Thro' the lone brake that shades thy mossy nest;
And shepherd girls, from eyes profane shall hide
   The gentle bird, who sings of pity best:
For still thy voice shall soft affections move,
And still be dear to sorrow, and to love!

SONNET VIII.

TO SPRING.

AGAIN the wood, and long with-drawing vale;
　　In many a tint of tender green are dreſt,
Where the young leaves unfolding, ſcarce conceal
　　Beneath their early ſhade, the half-form'd neſt
Of finch or wood-lark; and the primroſe pale,
　　And laviſh cowſlip, wildly ſcatter'd round,
Give their ſweet ſpirits to the ſighing gale.
　　Ah! ſeaſon of delight!——could aught be found
　　　To ſoothe awhile the tortur'd boſom's pain,
　　Of Sorrow's rankling ſhaft to cure the wound,
　　　And bring life's firſt deluſions once again,
'Twere ſurely met in thee!——thy proſpect fair,
Thy ſounds of harmony, thy balmy air,
Have power to cure all ſadneſs——but deſpair. 14

SONNET

SONNET IX.

BLEST is yon shepherd, on the turf reclin'd,
  Who on the varied clouds which float above
Lies idly gazing——while his vacant mind
  Pours out some tale antique of rural love!
  Ah! *he* has never felt the pangs that move
Th' indignant spirit, when with selfish pride,
  Friends, on whose faith the trusting heart rely'd,
    Unkindly shun th' imploring eye of woe!
  The ills they ought to soothe, with taunts deride,
    And laugh at tears themselves have forc'd to flow. 10
Nor *his* rude bosom those fine feelings melt,
  Children of Sentiment and Knowledge born,
Thro' whom each shaft with cruel force is felt,
  Empoison'd by deceit——or barb'd with scorn.

SONNET X.

TO MRS. G.

AH! why will Mem'ry with officious care
　　The long loft vifions of my days renew;
Why paint the vernal landfcape green and fair,
　　When life's gay dawn was opening to my view;
Ah! wherefore bring thofe moments of delight,
　　When with my Anna, on the fouthern fhore,
I thought the future, as the prefent bright;
　　Ye dear delufions!——ye return no more!
Alas! how diff'rent does the truth appear,
　　From the warm picture youth's rafh hand pourtrays
How fades the fcene, as we approach it near,
　　And pain and forrow ftrike——how many ways!
Yet of that tender heart, ah! ftill retain
A fhare for me——and I will not complain!——

SONNET

SONNET XI.

TO SLEEP.

COME balmy Sleep! tir'd nature's soft resort!
  On these sad temples all thy poppies shed;
And bid gay dreams, from Morpheus' airy court,
  Float in light vision round my aching head!
Secure of all thy blessings, partial Power!
  On his hard bed the peasant throws him down;
And the poor sea boy, in the rudest hour, 7
  Enjoys thee more than he who wears a crown.
Clasp'd in her faithful shepherd's guardian arms,
  Well may the village girl sweet slumbers prove;
And they, O gentle sleep!——still taste thy charms,
  Who wake to labour, liberty, and love.
But still thy opiate aid do'st thou deny
To calm the anxious breast; to close the streaming eye.

S O N N E T XII.

WRITTEN ON THE SEA SHORE.—OCTOBER, 1784.

On fome rude fragment of the rocky fhore,
  Where on the fractur'd cliff, the billows break,
  Mufing, my folitary feat I take,
And liften to the deep and folemn roar.

O'er the dark waves the winds tempeftuous howl;
  The fcreaming fea-bird quits the troubled fea:
  But the wild gloomy fcene has charms for me,
And fuits the mournful temper of my foul.   8

Already fhipwreck'd by the ftorms of Fate,
  Like the poor mariner methinks I ftand,
  Caft on a rock; who fees the diftant land
From whence no fuccour comes—or comes too late.
Faint and more faint are heard his feeble cries,
'Till! in the rifing tide, th' exhaufted fufferer dies.

S O N N E T

Plate 1.   Sonnet 8.

Stothard del.   Neagle sculp.

Published January 1.st 1789. by T. Cadell Strand.

On some rude fragment of the rocky shore.

SONNET XIII.

FROM PETRARCH.

OH! place me where the burning noon
  Forbids the wither'd flow'r to blow;
Or place me in the frigid zone,
  On mountains of eternal fnow:
Let me purfue the fteps of Fame,
  Or Poverty's more tranquil road;
Let youth's warm tide my veins inflame,
  Or fixty winters chill my blood:
Tho' my fond foul to Heav'n were flown,
  Or tho' on Earth 'tis doom'd to pine,
Prifoner or free—obfcure or known,
  My heart, oh Laura! ftill is thine.
Whate'er my deftiny may be,
That faithful heart, ftill burns for thee!

SONNET XIV.

FROM PETRARCH.

LOOSE to the wind her golden treffes ftream'd,
   Forming bright waves, with amorous Zephyr's fighs;
   And tho' averted now, her charming eyes
Then with warm love, and melting pity beam'd.
Was I deceiv'd?—Ah! furely, nymph divine!
   That fine fuffufion on thy cheek, was love;
   What wonder then thofe beauteous tints fhould move,
Should fire this heart, this tender heart of mine!
Thy foft melodious voice, thy air, thy fhape,
   Were of a goddefs——not a mortal maid;
   Yet tho' thy charms, thy heavenly charms fhould fade,
My heart, my tender heart could not efcape;
   Nor cure for me in time or change be found:
   The fhaft extracted, does not cure the wound!

SONNET

SONNET XV.

FROM PETRARCH.

WHERE the green leaves exclude the fummer beam,
  And foftly bend as balmy breezes blow,
And where, with liquid lapfe, the lucid ftream
  Acrofs the fretted rock is heard to flow,
Penfive I lay: when fhe whom Earth conceals,
  As if ftill living, to my eyes appears,
And pitying Heaven her angel form reveals,
  To fay——' Unhappy Petrarch, dry your tears;
' Ah! why fad lover! thus before your time,
  ' In grief and fadnefs fhould your life decay,
' And like a blighted flower, your manly prime
  ' 'In vain and hopelefs forrow, fade away?
' Ah! yield not thus to culpable defpair,
' But raife thine eyes to Heaven——and think I wait
     thee there.'

S O N N E T   XVI.

F R O M   P E T R A R C H.

Y E vales and woods! fair fcenes of happier hours!
 Ye feather'd people, tenants of the grove!
And you, bright ftream! befring'd with fhrubs and flowers,
 Behold my grief, ye witneffes of love!

For ye beheld my infant paffion rife,
 And faw thro' years unchang'd my faithful flame;
Now cold, in duft, the beauteous object lies,
 And you, ye confcious fcences, are ftill the fame!

While bufy memory ftill delights to dwell
 On all the charms thefe bitter tears deplore,
And with a trembling hand defcribes too well
 The angel form I fhall behold no more!
'To Heaven fhe's fled! and nought to me remains
But the pale afhes, which her urn contains.

S O N N E T

SONNET XVII.

FROM THE THIRTEENTH CANTATA OF METASTASIO.

ON thy grey bark, in witnefs of my flame,
   I carve Miranda's cypher——Beauteous tree !
Grac'd with the lovely letters of her name,
   Henceforth be facred, to my love and me !
Tho' the tall elm, the oak, and darker pine,
   With broader arms, may noon's fierce ardors break,
To fhelter me, and her I love, be thine ;
   And thine to fee her fmile and hear her fpeak.
No bird, ill omen'd, round thy graceful head
   Shall clamour harfh, or wave his heavy wing,
But fern and flowers arife beneath thy fhade,
   Where the wild bees, their lullabies fhall fing.
And in thy boughs the murmuring Ring-dove reft ;
And there the Nightingale fhall build her neft.

SONNET XVIII.

TO THE EARL OF EGREMONT.

WYNDHAM! 'tis not thy blood, tho' pure it runs
  Thro' a long line of glorious anceſtry,
Percys and Seymours, Britain's boaſted ſons,
  Who truſt the honors of their race to thee:

'Tis not thy ſplendid domes, where ſcience loves
  To touch the canvas, and the buſt to raiſe;
Thy rich domains, fair fields, and ſpreading groves;
  'Tis not all theſe the Muſe delights to praiſe!

In birth and wealth and honors, great thou art!
  But nobler, in thy independant mind;
And in that liberal hand and feeling heart
  Given thee by Heaven——a bleſſing to mankind!
Unworthy oft may titled fortune be;
A ſoul like thine——is true Nobility!

SONNET

SONNET XIX.

TO MR. HAYLEY.

ON RECEIVING SOME ELEGANT LINES FROM HIM.

FOR me the Mufe a fimple band defign'd
  Of ' idle' flowers, that bloom the woods among,
Which with the cyprefs and the willow join'd,
  A garland form'd, as artlefs as my fong.
And little dar'd I hope its tranfient hours
  So long would laft; compos'd of buds fo brief;
'Till Hayley's hand among the vagrant flowers,
  Threw from his verdant crown, a deathlefs leaf.
For high in Fame's bright fane has Judgment plac'd
  The laurel wreath Serena's poet won,
Which, wov'n with myrtles by the hands of Tafte,
  The Mufe decreed, for this her favourite fon.
And thofe immortal leaves his temples fhade,
Whofe fair eternal verdure—fhall not fade!

SONNET XX.

TO THE COUNTESS OF A————.

WRITTEN ON THE ANNIVERSARY OF HER MARRIAGE.

ON this bleſt day may no dark cloud or ſhower,
   With envious ſhade, the Sun's bright influence hide;
But all his rays illume the favour'd hour,
   That ſaw thee, Mary!————Henry's lovely bride!

With years revolving may it ſtill ariſe,
   Bleſt with each good approving Heaven can lend!
And ſtill with ray ſerene, ſhall thoſe blue eyes
   Enchant the huſband, and attach the friend!

For you, fair Friendſhip's amaranth ſhall blow,
   And Love's own thornleſs roſes, bind your brow!
And when—long hence—to happier worlds you go,
   Your beauteous race ſhall be, what you are now!
And future Nevills, thro' long ages ſhine,
With hearts as good, and forms as fair as thine!

SONNET

SONNET XXI.

SUPPOSED TO BE WRITTEN BY WERTER.

Go! cruel tyrant of the human breaſt!

  To other hearts, thy burning arrows bear;

Go, where fond hope, and fair illuſion reſt!

  Ah! why ſhould love inhabit with deſpair!

Like the poor maniac I linger here,   5

  Still haunt the ſcene, where all my treaſure lies;

Still ſeek for flowers, where only thorns appear,

  ' And drink delicious poiſon from her eyes!'   8

Towards the deep gulph that opens on my ſight

  I hurry forward, paſſion's helpleſs ſlave!

And ſcorning reaſon's mild and ſober light,

  Purſue the path that leads me to the grave!

So round the flame the giddy inſect flies,

And courts the fatal fire, by which it dies!

SONNET XXII.

BY THE SAME.

TO SOLITUDE.

OH, Solitude; to thy fequefter'd vale   1
  I come to hide my forrow and my tears,
And to thy echoes tell the mournful tale
  Which fcarce I truft to pitying Friendfhip's ears!
Amidft thy wild-woods, and untrodden glades,
  No founds but thofe of melancholy move;
And the low winds that die among thy fhades,
  Seem like foft Pity's fighs, for hopelefs love!
And fure fome ftory of defpair and pain,
  In yon deep copfe, thy murm'ring doves relate;
And hark! methinks in that long plaintive ftrain,
  Thine own fweet fongftrefs weeps my wayward fate!
Ah, Nymph! that fate affift me to endure,
And bear awhile——what death alone can cure!

SONNET

SONNET XXIII.

BY THE SAME.

TO THE NORTH STAR.

To thy bright beams I turn my fwimming eyes, :
  Fair, fav'rite planet! which in happier days
Saw my young hopes, ah! faithlefs hopes!—arife;
  And on my paffion fhed propitious rays!
Now nightly wandering mid the tempefts drear
  That howl the woods, and rocky fteeps among,
I love to fee thy fudden light appear
  Thro' the fwift clouds—driv'n by the wind along:
Or in the turbid water, rude and dark,
  O'er whofe wild ftream the guft of Winter raves,
Thy trembling light with pleafure ftill I mark,
  Gleam in faint radiance on the foaming waves!
So o'er my foul fhort rays of reafon fly,
Then fade:—and leave me, to defpair and die!

SONNET XXIV.

BY THE SAME.

MAKE there my tomb; beneath the lime-trees ſhade,
  Where graſs and flowers, in wild luxuriance wave;
Let no memorial mark where I am laid,
  Or point to common eyes the lover's grave!
But oft at twilight morn, or cloſing day,
  The faithful friend, with fault'ring ſtep ſhall glide,
Tributes of fond regret by ſtealth to pay,
  And ſigh o'er the unhappy ſuicide!
And ſometimes, when the Sun with parting rays
  Gilds the long graſs that hides my ſilent bed,
The tear ſhall tremble in my CHARLOTTE's eyes;
  Dear, precious drops!—they ſhall embalm the dead!
Yes!—CHARLOTTE o'er the mournful ſpot ſhall weep,
  Where her poor WERTER—and his ſorrows ſleep.

SONNET

SONNET XXV.

WHY fhould I wifh to hold in this low fphere 1
   ' A frail and feverifh being ?' wherefore try
Poorly from day to day to linger here,
    Againft the powerful hand of deftiny ?
By thofe who know the force of hopelefs care,
   On the worn heart—I fure fhall be forgiven,
If to elude dark gilt, and dire defpair,
   I go uncall'd—to mercy and to Heaven!
Oh thou! to fave whofe peace I now depart,
   Will thy foft mind, thy poor loft friend deplore,
When worms fhall feed on this devoted heart, 11
   Where even thy image fhall be found no more?
Yet may thy pity mingle not with pain,
For then thy haplefs lover—dies in vain!

SONNET

SONNET XXVI.

TO THE RIVER ARUN.

ON thy wild banks, by frequent torrents worn,
 No glittering fanes, or marble domes appear,
Yet shall the mournful muse thy course adorn,
 And still to her thy rustic waves be dear.
For with the infant Otway, lingering here, 5
 Of early woes she bade her votary dream,
While thy low murmurs soothed his pensive ear,
 And still the poet—consecrates the stream.
Beneath the oak and birch, that fringe thy side,
 The first-born violets of the year shall spring,
And in thy hazles, bending o'er the tide,
 The earliest Nightingale delight to sing:
While kindred spirits, pitying, shall relate
'Thy Otway's sorrows, and lament his fate!

SONNET

Plate 3.   Sonnet 26.

Stothard del.   Thornthwaite sculp.

Published Jany. 1.1789.by T.Cadell Strand.

For with the infant Oway lingering here

SONNET XXVII.

SIGHING I fee yon little troop at play;
  By forrow yet untouch'd; unhurt by care;
While free and fportive they enjoy to-day,
  'Content and carelefs of to-morrow's fare!'   4
O happy age! when Hope's unclouded ray
  Lights their green path, and prompts their fimple mirth,
E'er yet they feel the thorns that lurking lay
  To wound the wretched pilgrims of the earth,
Making them rue the hour that gave them birth,
  And threw them on a world fo full of pain,
Where profperous folly treads on patient worth,
  And to deaf pride, misfortune pleads in vain!
Ah!—for their future fate how many fears
Opprefs my heart—and fill mine eyes with tears!

SONNET

SONNET XXVIII.

TO FRIENDSHIP.

OH thou! whose name too often is profan'd!
  Whose charms, celestial! few have hearts to feel!
Unknown to folly—and by pride disdain'd!
  —To thy soft solace may my sorrows steal!
Like the fair Moon, thy mild and genuine ray,
  Thro' life's long evening shall unclouded last;
While pleasure's frail attachments fleet away,
  As fades the rainbow from the northern blast!
Tis thine, oh Nymph! with 'balmy hands to bind'
  The wounds inflicted in misfortune's storm,
    And blunt severe affliction's sharpest dart!
—'Tis thy pure spirit warms my Anna's mind,
  Beams thro' the pensive softness of her form,
    And holds its altar—on her spotless heart!

SONNET XXIX.

TO MISS C——

ON BEING DESIRED TO ATTEMPT WRITING A COMEDY.

WOULD'ST thou then have *me* tempt the comic fcene
 Of gay Thalia? Us'd fo long to tread
 The gloomy paths of forrow's cyprefs fhade;
And the lorn lay, with fighs and tears to ftain?
Alas! how much unfit her fprightly vein!
 Arduous to try!—and feek the funny mead,
 And bowers of rofes, where fhe loves to lead.
The fportive fubjects of her golden reign!
Enough for me, if ftill, to foothe my days,
 Her fair and penfive fifter condefcend,
With tearful fmile to blefs my fimple lays;
 Enough, if her foft notes fhe fometimes lend,.
To gain for me, of feeling hearts the praife,
 And chiefly thine, my ever partial friend!

SONNET

S O N N E T   XXX.

TO THE RIVER ARUN.

BE the proud Thames, of trade the bufy mart!
  Arun! to thee will other praife belong;
Dear to the lover's, and the mourner's heart,
  And ever facred to the fons of fong!

Thy banks romantic, hopelefs Love fhall feek,
  Where o'er the rocks the mantling bind with flaunts; 6
And Sorrows drooping form and faded cheek,
  Chcofe on thy willow'd fhore her lonely haunts!

Banks! which infpir'd thy Otway's plaintive ftrain! 9
  Wilds!—whofe lorn echo's learn'd the deeper tone
Of Collins' powerful fhell! yet once again
  Another poet—Hayley is thine own!
Thy claffic ftream anew fhall hear a lay,
Bright as its waves, and various as its way!

SONNET

SONNET XXXI.

SPRING'S dewy hand on this fair fummit weaves
   The downy grafs, with tufts of Alpine flowers, ²
And fhades the beechen flopes with tender leaves,
   And leads the fhepherd to his upland bowers,
Strewn with wild thyme; while flow-defcending fhowers,
   Feed the green ear, and nurfe the future fheaves!
   —Ah! bleft the hind—whom no fad thought bereaves
Of the gay Seafon's pleafures!—All his hours
To wholefome labour given, or thoughtlefs mirth;
   No pangs of forrow paft, or coming dread,
Bend his unconfcious fpirit down to earth,
   Or chafe calm flumbers from his carelefs head!
Ah! what to me can thofe dear days reftore,
When fcenes could charm, that now I tafte no more!

SONNET

SONNET XXXII.

TO MELANCHOLY.

WRITTEN ON THE BANKS OF THE ARUN, OCTOBER, 1785.

WHEN lateſt Autumn ſpreads her evening veil
   And the grey miſts from theſe dim waves ariſe,
   I love to liſten to the hollow ſighs,
Thro' the half leafleſs wood that breathes the gale.
For at ſuch hours the ſhadowy phantom, pale.
   Oft ſeems to fleet before the poet's eyes;
   Strange ſounds are heard, and mournful melodies,
As of night wanderers, who their woes bewail!
Here, by his native ſtream, at ſuch an hour,
   Pity's own Otway, I methinks could meet,
     And hear his deep ſighs ſwell the ſadden'd wind!
Oh Melancholy!—ſuch thy magic power,
   That to the ſoul theſe dreams are often ſweet,
     And ſoothe the penſive viſionary mind!

SONNET

SONNET XXXIII.

TO THE NAIAD OF THE ARUN.

Go! rural Naiad; wind thy stream along
  Thro' woods and wilds: then seek the ocean caves
Where sea nymphs meet, their coral rocks among,
  To boast the various honors of their waves!
'Tis but a little, o'er thy shallow tide,
  That toiling trade her burthen'd vessel leads;
But laurels grow luxuriant on thy side,
  And letters live, along thy classic meads.
Lo! where 'mid British bards thy natives shine!   9
  And now another poet helps to raise
Thy glory high——the poet of the MINE!
  Whose brilliant talents are his smallest praise:
And who, to all that genius can impart,
Adds the cool head, and the unblemish'd heart!

SONNET XXXIV.

TO A FRIEND.

CHARM'D by thy fuffrage, fhall I yet afpire,
  (All inaufpicious as my fate appears,
  By troubles darken'd, that increafe with years,)
To guide the crayon, or to touch the lyre?
Ah me!——the fifter Mufes ftill require
  A fpirit free from all intrufive fears,
  Nor will they deign to wipe away the tears
Of vain regret, that dim their facred fire.
But when thy envied fanction crowns my lays,
  A ray of pleafure lights my languid mind,
For well I know the value of thy praife;
  And to how few, the flattering meed confin'd,
  That thou,—their highly favour'd brows to bind,
Wilt weave green myrtle, and unfading bays!

SONNET

SONNET XXXV.

TO FORTITUDE.

NYMPH of the rock! whofe dauntlefs fpirit braves
   The beating ftorm, and bitter winds that howl
Round thy cold breaft; and hear'ft the burfting waves,
   And the deep thunder with unfhaken foul;
Oh come!—and fhew how vain the cares that prefs
   On my weak bofom—and how little worth
Is the falfe fleeting meteor, happinefs,
   That ftill mifleads the wanderers of the earth!
Strengthen'd by thee, this heart fhall ceafe to melt
   O'er ills that poor humanity muft bear;
Nor friends eftrang'd, or ties diffolv'd be felt
   To leave regret, and fruitlefs anguifh there:
And when at length it heaves its lateft figh,
Thou and mild hope, fhall teach me how to die!

SONNET XXXVI.

SHOULD the lone Wanderer, fainting on his way,
   Reſt for a moment of the ſultry hours,
And tho' his path thro' thorns and roughneſs lay,
   Pluck the wild roſe, or woodbine's gadding flowers;
Weaving gay wreaths, beneath ſome ſheltering tree,
   The ſenſe of ſorrow, he awhile may loſe;
So have I ſought thy flowers, fair Poeſy!
   So charm'd my way, with Friendſhip and the Muſe.
But darker now grows life's unhappy day,
   Dark, with new clouds of evil, yet to come,
Her pencil ſickening Fancy throws away,
   And weary Hope reclines upon the tomb;
And points my wiſhes to that tranquil ſhore,
Where the pale ſpectre Care, purſues no more.

Corbould del   Naigle sculp

Published as the Act directs by T. Cadell Strand Jan.r 1, 1789.

Her pencil sickening fancy throws away

And weary hope reclines upon the tomb.

SONNET XXXVII.

THE poet's fancy takes from Flora's realm
   Her buds and leaves to drefs fictitious powers,
With the green olive fhades Minerva's helm,
   And gives to Beauty's Queen, the Queen of flowers.
But what gay bloffoms of luxuriant Spring,
   With rofe, mimofa, amaranth entwin'd,
Shall fabled Sylphs, and fairy people bring,
   As a juft emblem of the lovely mind?
In vain the mimic pencil tries to blend
   The glowing dyes that drefs the flowery race,
   Scented and colour'd by an hand divine!
Ah! not lefs vainly would the Mufe pretend
   On her weak lyre, to fing the native grace
   And native goodnefs of a foul like thine!

SONNET XXXVIII.

FROM THE NOVEL OF EMMELINE.

WHEN welcome flumber fets my fpirit free,
  Forth to fictitious happinefs it flies,
  And where Elyfian bowers of blifs arife
I feem, my Emmeline—to meet with thee!
Ah! Fancy then, diffolving human ties,
  Gives me the wifhes of my foul to fee;
Tears of fond pity fill thy foftened eyes;
  In heavenly harmony—our hearts agree.
Alas! thefe joys are mine in dreams alone,
When cruel Reafon abdicates her throne!
  Her harfh return condemns me to complain
Thro' life unpitied, unrelieved, unknown.
  And as the dear delufions leave my brain,
  She bids the truth recur—with aggravated pain.

SONNET XXXIX.

TO NIGHT.

FROM THE SAME.

I LOVE thee, mournful fober-fuited night,
　When the faint moon, yet lingering in her wane,
And veil'd in clouds, with pale uncertain light
　Hangs o'er the waters of the reftlefs main.
In deep depreffion funk, the enfeebled mind
　Will to the deaf, cold elements complain,
　And tell the embofom'd grief, however vain,
To fullen furges and the viewlefs wind.
Tho' no repofe on thy dark breaft I find,
　I ftill enjoy thee—cheerlefs as thou art;
　For in thy quiet gloom, the exhaufted heart
Is calm, tho' wretched; hopelefs, yet refign'd.
While, to the winds and waves its forrows given,
May reach—tho' loft on earth—the car of Heaven!

SONNET XL.

FROM THE SAME.

FAR on the fands, the low, retiring tide,
  In diftant murmurs hardly feems to flow,
And o'er the world of waters, blue and wide,
  The fighing fummer wind, forgets to blow.
As finks the day ftar in the rofy Weft,
  The filent wave, with rich reflection glows;
Alas! can tranquil nature give *me* reft,
  Or fcenes of beauty, foothe me to repofe?
Can the foft luftre of the fleeping main,
  Yon radient heaven, or all creation's charms,
" Erafe the written troubles of the brain,"
  Which Memory tortures, and which guilt alarms?
Or bid a bofom tranfient quiet prove,
That bleeds with vain remorfe, and unextinguifh'd love!

SONNET

SONNET XLI.

TO TRANQUILLITY.

IN this tumultuous fphere, for thee unfit,
   How feldom art thou found——Tranquillity!
   Unlefs 'tis when with mild and downcaft eye
By the low cradles, thou delight'ft to fit,
Of fleeping infants——watching the foft breath,
   And bidding the fweet flumberers eafy lie;
Or fometimes hanging o'er the bed of death,
   Where the poor languid fufferer——hopes to die.
Oh! beauteous fifter of the halcyon peace!
   I fure fhall find thee in that heavenly fcene
      Where care and anguifh fhall their power refign;
Where hope alike, and vain regret fhall ceafe;
   And Memory—loft in happinefs ferene,
      Repeat no more—that mifery has been mine!

SONNET

S O N N E T XLII.

COMPOSED DURING A WALK ON THE DOWNS,
IN NOVEMBER 1787.

THE dark and pillowy cloud; the fallow trees,
Seem o'er the ruins of the year to mourn;
And cold and hollow, the inconstant breeze
Sobs thro' the falling leaves and wither'd fern.
O'er the tall brow of yonder chalky bourn,
The evening-shades their gather'd darkness fling,
While, by the lingering light, I scarce discern
The shrieking night-jar, sail on heavy wing. s
Ah! yet a little——and propitious Spring
Crown'd with fresh flowers, shall wake the woodland
    strain;
But no gay change revolving seasons bring,
To call forth pleasure from the soul of pain,
Bid Syren Hope resume her long lost part,
And chase the vulture Care—that feeds upon the heart.

S O N N E T

SONNET XLIII.

THE unhappy exile, whom his fates confine
 To the bleak coaſt of ſome unfriendly iſle,
 Cold, barren, deſart, where no harveſts ſmile,
But thirſt and hunger on the rocks repine;
When, from ſome promontory's fearful brow,
 Sun after ſun he hopeleſs ſees decline
In the broad ſhipleſs ſea——perhaps may know
 Such heartleſs pain, ſuch blank deſpair as mine;
And, if a flattering cloud appears to ſhow
 The fancied ſemblance of a diſtant ſail,
 Then melts away——anew his ſpirits fail,
While the loſt hope but aggravates his woe!
Ah! ſo for me deluſive Fancy toils,
Then, from contraſted truth—my feeble ſoul recoils.

SONNET XLIV.

PRESS'D by the Moon, mute arbitrefs of tides,
  While the loud equinox its power combines,
  The fea no more its fwelling furge confines,
But o'er the fhrinking land fublimely rides.
The wild blaft, rifing from the Weftern cave,
  Drives the huge billows from their heaving bed;
  Tears from their graffy tombs the village dead, 7
And breaks the filent fabbath of the grave!
With fhells and fea-weed mingled, on the fhore
  Lo! their bones whiten in the frequent wave;
  But vain to them the winds and waters rave;
They hear the warring elements no more:
While I am doom'd—by life's long ftorm oppreft,
To gaze with envy, on their gloomy reft.

SONNET XLV.

ON LEAVING A PART OF SUSSEX.

FAREWELL Aruna!—on whofe varied fhore
My early vows were paid to Nature's fhrine,
When thoughtlefs joy, and infant hope were mine,
And whofe lorn ftream has heard me fince deplore
Too many forrows!   Sighing I refign
Thy folitary beauties—and no more
Or on thy rocks, or in thy woods recline,
Or on the heath, by moon-light lingering, pore
On air-drawn phantoms——While in Fancy's ear
As in the evening wind thy murmurs fwell,
The Enthufiaft of the Lyre, who wander'd here, 11'
Seems yet to ftrike his vifionary fhell,
Of power to call forth Pity's tendereft tear
Or wake wild frenzy——from her hideous cell!

SONNET XLVI.

WRITTEN AT PENSHURST, IN AUTUMN 1788.

YE Towers fublime, deferted now and drear,
  Ye woods, deep fighing to the hollow blaft,
The mufing wanderer loves to linger near,
  While Hiftory points to all your glories paft :
And ftartling from their haunts the timid deer,
  To trace the walks obfcured by matted fern,
Which Waller's foothing lyre were wont to hear,
  But where now clamours the difcordant heron ! S
The fpoiling hand of Time may overturn
  Thefe lofty battlements, and quite deface
The fading canvas whence we love to learn
  Sydney's keen look, and Sachariffa's grace ;
But fame and beauty ftill defy decay,
Saved by the hiftoric page——the poet's tender lay !

SONNET XLVII.

TO FANCY.

THEE, Queen of Shadows!—fhall I ftill invoke,
Still love the fcenes thy fportive pencil drew,
When on mine eyes the early radience broke
Which fhew'd the beauteous, rather than the true!
Alas! long fince, thofe glowing tints are dead,
And now 'tis thine in darkeft hues to drefs
The fpot where pale Experience hangs her head
O'er the fad grave of murder'd Happinefs!
Thro' thy falfe medium then, no longer view'd,
May fancied pain and fancied pleafure fly,
And I, as from me all thy dreams depart,
Be to my wayward deftiny fubdu'd;
Nor feek perfection with a poet's eye,
Nor fuffer anguifh with a poet's heart!

SONNET XLVIII.

TO MRS. * * * *

No more my wearied foul attempts to ftray
From fad reality and vain regret,
Nor courts enchanting fiction to allay
Sorrows that fenfe refufes to forget :
For of calamity fo long the prey,
Imagination now has loft her powers,
Nor will her fairy loom again effay
To drefs affliction in a robe of flowers.
But if no more the bowers of Fancy bloom
Let one fuperior fcene attract my view,
Where heav'ns pure rays the facred fpot illume,
Let *thy* lov'd hand with palm and amaranth ftrew
The mournful path approaching to the tomb,
While Faith's confoling voice endears the friendly gloom.

ODE TO DESPAIR.

FROM THE NOVEL OF EMMELINE.

THOU spectre of terrific mien,
Lord of the hopeless heart and hollow eye,
In whose fierce train each form is seen
That drives sick Reason to insanity!
I woo thee with unusual prayer,
" Grim visaged, comfortless Despair :"
Approach ; in me a willing victim find,
Who seeks thine iron sway—and calls thee kind !

Ah! hide for ever from my sight
The faithless flatterer Hope—whose pencil, gay,
Portrays some vision of delight,
Then bids the fairy tablet fade away ;
While in dire contrast, to mine eyes
Thy phantoms, yet more hideous, rise,

E   And

And Memory draws, from Pleafure's wither'd flower,
Corrofives for the heart—of fatal power!

I bid the traitor Love, adieu!
Who to this fond, believing bofom came,
A gueft infidious and untrue,
With Pity's foothing voice—in Friendfhip's name;
The wounds *he* gave, nor Time fhall cure
Nor Reafon teach me to endure.
And to that breaft mild Patience pleads in vain,
Which feels the curfe—of meriting it's pain.

Yet not to me, tremendous power!
Thy worft of fpirit-wounding pangs impart,
With which, in dark conviction's hour,
Thou ftrik'ft the guilty unrepentant heart!
But of illufion long the fport,
That dreary, tranquil gloom I court,
Where my paft errors I may ftill deplore
And dream of long-loft happinefs no more!

To

To thee I give this tortured breaſt,

Where Hope ariſes but to foſter pain;

Ah! lull it's agonies to reſt!

Ah! let me never be deceiv'd again!

But callous, in thy deep repoſe

Behold, in long array, the woes

Of the dread future, calm and undiſmay'd,

Till I may claim the Hope—that ſhall not fade!

E 2   ELEGY.

E L E G Y. 1

DARK gathering clouds involve the threatening
    ſkies,
' The ſea heaves conſcious of the impending gloom,
' Deep, hollow murmurs from the cliffs ariſe ;
' They come—the Spirits of the Tempeſt come !

' Oh ! may ſuch terrors mark the approaching night
' As reign'd on that theſe ſtreaming eyes deplore !
' Flaſh, ye red fires of heaven, with fatal light,
' And with conflicting winds, ye waters roar !

' Loud and more loud ye foaming billows burſt !
' Ye warring elements more fiercely rave !
' Till the wide waves o'erwhelm the ſpot accurſt
" Where ruthleſs Avarice finds a quiet grave !"

Thus

Plate 5.

Elegy

Corbould del.

Heath sculp.

Published Jan.ʳ 1 1789. by T. Cadell Strand.

Thus with clafp'd hands, wild looks, and ftreaming hair,
While fhrieks of horror broke her trembling fpeech,
A wretched maid—the victim of defpair,
Survey'd the threatening ftorm and defart beech,

Then to the tomb where now the father flept
Whofe rugged nature bade her forrows flow,
Frantic fhe turn'd—and beat her breaft and wept,
Invoking vengeance on the duft below.

' Lo! rifing there above each humbler heap,
' Yon cypher'd ftones *his* name and wealth relate,
' Who gave his fon—remorfelefs—to the deep,
' While I, his living victim, curfe my fate.

' Oh! my loft love! no tomb is plac'd for thee,
' That may to ftrangers eyes thy worth impart ;
' Thou haft no grave, but in the ftormy fea,
' And no memorial but this breaking heart.

• Forth

' Forth to the world, a widow'd wanderer driven,

' I pour to winds and waves the unheeded tear,

' Try with vain effort to fubmit to heaven,

' And fruitlefs call on him—" who cannot hear."

' Oh ! might I fondly clafp him once again,

' While o'er my head the infuriate billows pour,

Forget in death this agonizing pain,

And feel his father's cruelty no more!

' Part, raging waters part, and fhew beneath,

' In your dread caves, his pale and mangled form ;

' Now, while the demons of defpair and death

' Ride on the blaft, and urge the howling ftorm !

' Lo! by the lightenings momentary blaze,

' I fee him rife the whitening waves above,

' No longer fuch as when in happier days

' He gave the enchanted hours—to me and love.

' Such, as when daring the enchafed fea,

' And courting dangerous toil, he often faid,

' That every peril, one foft fmile from me,

' One figh of fpeechlefs tendernefs, o'erpaid.

' But dead, disfigur'd, while between the roar

' Of the loud waves his accents pierce mine ear,

' And feem to fay——Ah! wretch, delay no more,

' But come, unhappy mourner—meet me here.

' Yet powerful fancy bid the phantom ftay,

' Still let me hear him !—'Tis already paft;

' Along the waves his fhadow glides away,

' I lofe his voice amid the deafening blaft.

' Ah! wild illufion, born of frantic pain !

' He hears not, comes not from his watery bed ;

' My tears, my anguifh, my defpair are vain,

' The infatiate ocean gives not up its dead.

Tis

' 'Tis not his voice! Hark! the deep thunders roll;

' Up-heaves the ground; the rocky barriers fail;

' Approach, ye horrors that delight my foul,

' Defpair, and Death, and Defolation, hail!' ·

The ocean hears——The embodied waters come—

Rife o'er the land, and with refiftlefs fweep

Tear from it's bafe the proud aggreffor's tomb,

And bear the injured to eternal fleep!

SONG

S O N G.

FROM THE FRENCH OF CARDINAL BERNIS.

I.

FRUIT of Aurora's tears, fair rofe,
  On whofe foft leaves fond Zephyrs play,
Oh! queen of flowers, thy buds difclofe,
  And give thy fragrance to the day;
Unveil thy tranfient charms:——ah, no!
  A little be thy bloom delay'd,
Since the fame hour that bids thee blow
  Shall fee thee droop thy languid head.

II.

But go! and on Themira's breaft
  Find, happy flower, thy throne and tomb;
While, jealous of a fate fo bleft,
  How fhall I envy thee thy doom!

Should

Should fome rude hand approach thee there,

 Guard the fweet fhrine thou wilt adorn;

Ah! punifh thofe who rafhly dare,

 And for my rivals keep thy thorn.

III.

Love fhall himfelf thy boughs compofe,

 And bid thy wanton leaves divide;

He'll fhew thee how, my lovely rofe,

 To deck her bofom, not to hide:

And thou fhalt tell the cruel maid

 How frail are youth and beauty's charms,

And teach her, ere her own fhall fade,

 To give them to her lover's arms.

THE

THE

ORIGIN OF FLATTERY.

WHEN Jove, in anger to the fons of earth,
Bid artful Vulcan give Pandora birth,
And fent the fatal gift, which fpread below
O'er all the wretched race contagious woe,
Unhappy man, by vice and folly toft,
Found in the ftorms of life his quiet loft,
While Envy, Avarice, and Ambition, hurl'd
Difcord and death around the warring world;
Then the bleft peafant left his fields and fold,
And barter'd love and peace, for power and gold;
Left his calm cottage, and his native plain,
In fearch of wealth to tempt the faithlefs main;
Or, braving danger, in the battle ftood,
And bath'd his favage hands in human blood:

No

No longer then, his woodland walks among,
The fhepherd lad his genuine. paffion fung,
Or fought at early morn his foul's delight,
Or grav'd her name upon the bark at night;
To deck her flowing hair no more he wove
The fimple wreath, or with ambitious love
Bound his own brow with myrtle or with bay,
But broke his pipe, and threw his crook away.
The nymphs forfaken, other pleafures fought;
Then firft for gold their venal hearts were bought,
And nature's blufh to fickly art gave place,
And affectation feiz'd the feat of grace:
No more fimplicity, by fenfe refin'd,
Or generous fentiment, poffefs'd the mind;
No more they felt each other's joy and woe,
And Cupid fled, and hid his ufelefs bow.
But with deep grief propitious Venus pin'd,
To fee the ills which threaten'd womankind;
Ills, that fhe knew her empire would difarm,
And rob her fubjects of their fweeteft charm;

Good

Good humour's potent influence deftroy,

And change for lowering frowns, the fmile of joy.

Then deeply fighing at the mournful view,

She try'd at length what heavenly art could do

To bring back pleafure to her penfive train,

And vindicate the glories of her reign.

A thoufand little loves attend the tafk,

And bear from Mars's head his radient cafque,

The fair enchantrefs on its filver bound,

Wreath'd with foft fpells her magic ceftus round,

Then fhaking from her hair ambrofial dew,

Infus'd fair hope, and expectation new,

And ftifled wifhes, and perfuafive fighs,

And fond belief, and ' eloquence of eyes,'

And fault'ring accents, which explain fo well

What ftudied fpeeches vainly try to tell,

And more pathetic filence, which imparts

Infectious tendernefs to feeling hearts,

Soft tones of pity; falcinating fmiles;

And Maia's fon affifted her with wiles,

And

And brought gay dreams, fantaftic vifions brought,

And wav'd his wand o'er the feducing draught.

Then Zephyr came: To him the goddefs cried,

‘ Go fetch from Flora all her flow'ry pride

‘ To fill my charm, each fcented bud that blows,

‘ And bind my myrtles with her thornlefs rofe;

‘ Then fpeed thy flight to Gallia's fmiling plain,

‘ Where rolls the Loire, the Garonne, and the Seine;

‘ Dip in their waters thy celeftial wing,

And the foft dew to fill my chalice bring;

But chiefly tell thy Flora, that to me

‘ She fend a bouquet of her fleurs de lys;

‘ That poignant fpirit will compleat my fpell.'

——'Tis done: the lovely forcerefs fays 'tis well.

And now Apollo lends a ray of fire,

The cauldron bubbles, and the flames afpire;

The watchful Graces round the circle dance,

With arms entwin'd, to mark the work's advance;

And with full quiver fportive Cupid came,

Temp'ring his favourite arrows in the flame.

Then

Then Venus fpeaks, the wavering flames retire,
And Zephyr's breath extinguifhes the fire.
At length the goddefs in the helmet's round
A fweet and fubtil fpirit duly found,
More foft than oil, than æther more refin'd,
Of power to cure the woes of womankind,
And called it Flattery :——balm of female life,
It charms alike the widow, maid, and wife;
Clears the fad brow of virgins in defpair,
And fmooths the cruel traces left by care;
Bids palfy'd age with youthful fpirit glow,
And hangs May's garlands on December's fnow.
Delicious effence! howfoe'er apply'd,
By what rude nature is thy charm deny'd?
Some form feducing ftill thy whifper wears,
Stern Wifdom turns to thee her willing ears,
And Prudery liftens, and forgets her fears.
The ruftic nymph, whom rigid aunts reftrain,
Condemn'd to drefs, and practife airs in vain,

At

At thy firſt ſummons finds her boſom ſwell,

And bids her crabbed gouvernantes farewell;

While, fir'd by thee with ſpirit not her own,

She grows a toaſt, and riſes into *ton*.

The faded beauty who with ſecret pain,

Sees younger charms uſurp her envied reign,

By thee aſſiſted, can with ſmiles behold

The record where her conqueſts are enroll'd;

And dwelling yet on ſcenes by memory nurs'd,

When George the Second reign'd, or George the Firſt;

She ſees the ſhades of ancient beaux ariſe,

Who ſwear her eyes exceeded modern eyes,

When poets ſung for her and lovers bled,

And giddy faſhion follow'd as ſhe led.

Departed modes appear in long array,

The flowers and flounces of her happier day,

Again her locks the decent fillets bind,

The waving lappet flutters in the wind,

And then comparing with a proud diſdain

The more fantaſtic taſtes that now obtain,

She

She deems ungraceful, trifling and abfurd,

The gayer world that moves round George the Third.

Nor thy foft influence will the train refufe,

Who court in diftant fhades the modeft Mufe,

Tho' in a form more pure and more refin'd,

Thy foothing fpirit meets the letter'd mind.

Not death itfelf thine empire can deftroy ;

Towards thee, even then, we turn the languid eye ;

Still truft in thee to bid our memory bloom,

And fcatter rofes round the filent tomb.

QUOTATIONS,

QUOTATIONS, NOTES,

and EXPLANATIONS.

S O N N E T   I.

LINE 13.

Ah! then, how dear the Mufe's favors coft,
If thofe paint forrow beft—who feel it moft!

The well fung woes fhall foothe my penfive ghoft;
He beft can paint them, who fhall feel them moft.

Pope's Eloifa to Abelard, 366th line.

S O N N E T   II.

LINE 3.

Anemonies, that fpangled every grove.
Anemony Nemerofo.   The wood Anemony.

SONNET

S O N N E T III.

LINE I.

The idea from the 43d Sonnet of Petrarch. Secondo parte.

Quel rofigniuol, che fi foave piagne.

S O N N E T V.

LINE 2.

Your turf, your flowers among.

Whofe turf, whofe fhades, whofe flowers among.

Gray.

LINE 9.

Aruna!

The river Arun.

S O N N E T VI.

LINE 12.

· For me the vernal garland blooms no more.'

Pope's Imit. 1ſt Ode 4th Book of Horace.

LINE

LINE 13.

' Mifery's love.'

Shakefpeare's King John.

S O N N E T VII.

LINE 4.

' On the night's dull ear.'

Shakefpeare.

LINE 5.

Whether on Spring—Alludes to the fuppofed migration of the Nightingale.

LINE 7.

The penfive Mufe fhall own thee for his mate.

Whether the Mufe or Love call thee his mate,
Both them I ferve, and of their train am I.

Milton's Firft Sonnet.

S O N N E T

S O N N E T   VIII.

LINE 14.

Have power to cure all fadnefs—but defpair!

To the heart infpires
Vernal delight and joy, able to drive
All fadnefs but defpair.

Paradife Loft, Fourth Book.

S O N N E T   IX.

LINE 10.

And laugh at tears themfelves have forc'd to flow.

And hard unkindnefs' alter'd eye,
That mocks the tear it forc'd to flow.

Gray.

S O N N E T   XI.

LINE 4.

Float in light vifion round my aching head.

Float in light vifion round the poet's head.

Mafon.

LINE

LINE 7.

And the poor fea boy, in the rudeft hour,
Enjoys thee more than he who wears a crown.

Wilt thou upon the high and giddy maft
Seal up the fhip boy's eyes, and rock his brains
In cradle of the rude impetuous furge? &c.

Shakefpeare's Henry IV.

S O N N E T   XII.

LINE 8.

And fuits the mournful temper of my foul.

Young.

S O N N E T   XIII.

LINE I.

Pommi ove'l Sol, occide i fiori e l'erba.

Petrarch, Sonnetto 112, Parte primo.

S O N N E T

S O N N E T   XIV.

LINE I.

Erano i capei d'oro all aura fparfi.

Sonnetto 69.   *Parte primo.*

S O N N E T   XV.

LINE I.

Se lamentar augelli o verdi fronde.

Sonnetto 21.   *Parte ficondo.*

S O N N E T   XVI.

LINE I.

Valle che de lamenti miei fe piena.

Sonnetto 33.   *Parte fecondo.*

S O N N E T   XVII.

LINE I.

Scrivo in te l'amato nome
Di colei, per cui, mi moro.

This

This is not meant as a tranflation ; the original is much longer, and full of images, which could not be introduced in a Sonnet.—And fome of them, tho' very beautiful in the Italian, would not appear to advantage in an Englifh drefs.

S O N N E T XXI.

LINE 5.

' Poor Maniac.'

See the Story of the Lunatic.

' Is this the deftiny of man ? Is he only happy before he poffeffes his reafon, or after he has loft it ?—Full of hope you go to gather flowers in Winter, and are grieved not to find any—and do not know why they cannot be found.'

Sorrows of Werter. Volume Second.

LINE 8.

' And drink delicious poifon from thine eye.'

Pope.

S O N N E T

S O N N E T XXII.

LINE I.

' I climb steep rocks, I break my way through copses, among thorns and briars which tear me to pieces, and I feel a little relief.'

Sorrows of Werter. Volume First.

S O N N E T XXIII.

LINE I.

' The greater Bear, favourite of all the constellations; for when I left you of an evening it us'd to shine opposite your window.'

Sorrows of Werter. Volume Second.

S O N N E T XXIV.

LINE I.

' At the corner of the church yard which looks towards the fields, there are two lime trees—it is there I wish to rest.'

Sorrows of Werter. Volume Second.

S O N N E T

S O N N E T   XXV.

LINE 1.

' May my death remove every obftacle to your happinefs.—Be at peace, I intreat you be at peace.'

Sorrows of Werter.   Volume Second.

LINE II.

When worms fhall feed on this devoted heart,
Where even thy image fhall be found no more.

From a line in Rouffeau's Eloifa.

S O N N E T   XXVI.

LINE 5.

For with the infant Otway, lingering here.

Otway was born at Trotten, a village in Suffex. Of Woolbeding, another village on the banks of the Arun, (which runs through them both,) his father was rector. Here it was therefore that he

probably

probably paſſed many of his early years. The Arun is here an inconſiderable ſtream, winding in a channel deeply worn, among meadow, heath, and wood.

S O N N E T   XXVII.

LINE 4.

' Content, and careleſs of to-morrow's fare.'

Thomſon.

S O N N E T   XXVIII.

LINE 9.

' Balmy hand to bind.'

Collins.

S O N N E T   XXX.

LINE 6.

Bindwith.

The plant Clematis, Bindwith, Virgin's Bower, or Travellers Joy, which towards the end of June

begins

begins to cover the hedges and sides of rocky hol-
lows, with its beautiful foliage, and flowers of a
yellowish white of an agreeable fragrance ; these
are succeeded by feed pods, that bear some resem-
blance to feathers or hair, whence it is sometimes
called Old Man's Beard.

LINE 9.

Banks! which inspir'd thy Otway's plaintive strain!
Wilds! whose lorn Echo's learn'd the deeper tone
Of Collins' powerful shell!

Collins, as well as Otway, was a native of this
country, and probably at some period of his life an
inhabitant of this neighbourhood, since in his beautiful Ode on the death of Colonel Rofs, he says:

The Muse shall still, with social aid,
Her gentlest promise keep,
E'en humble Harting's cottag'd vale
Shall learn the sad repeated tale,
And bid her shepherds weep.

And

And in the Ode to Pity:

> Wild Arun too has heard thy ſtrains,
> And Echo, midſt my native plains,
> Been ſooth'd with Pity's lute.

S O N N E T   XXXI.

LINE 2.

' Alpine flowers.'

An infinite variety of plants are found on theſe hills, particularly about this ſpot: many ſorts of Orchis and Ciſtus of ſingular beauty, with ſeveral others.

S O N N E T   XXXIII.

LINE 9.

Thy natives.

Otway, Collins, Hayley.

S O N N E T

S O N N E T   XLII.

LINE 8.

" The fhrieking night-jar fail on heavy wing."

The night-jar or night hawk, a dark bird not fo big as a rook, which is frequently feen of an evening on the downs. It has a fhort heavy flight, then refts on the ground, and again, uttering a mournful cry, flits before the traveller, to whom its appearance is fuppofed by the peafants to portend misfortune. As I have never feen it dead, I know not to what fpecies it belongs.

S O N N E T   XLIV.

LINE 7.

Middleton is a village on the margin of the fea in Suffex, containing only two or three houfes. There were formerly feveral acres of ground between its fmall church and the fea; which now,

by

by its continual encroachments, approaches within
a few feet of this half ruined and humble edifice.
The wall, which once furrounded the church yard,
is entirely fwept away, many of the graves broken
up, and the remains of bodies interred wafhed into
the fea: whence human bones are found among
the fand and fhingles on the fhore.

S O N N E T   XLV.

LINE 11.

" The enthufiaft of the lyre who wander'd here."

Collins.—See note to Sonnet 30.

S O N N E T   XLVI.

LINE 8.

" But where now clamours the difcordant heron."

In the park at Penfhurft is an heronry. The
houfe is at prefent uninhabited, and the windows
of the galleries and other rooms, in which there
are many invaluable pictures, are never opened
but when ftrangers vifit it.

LINE

Algernon Sidney.

E L E G Y.

This elegy is written on the fuppofition that an indigent young woman had been addreffed by the fon of a wealthy yeoman, who refenting his attachment, had driven him from home, and compelled him to have recourfe for fubfiftence to the occupation of a pilot, in which, attempting to fave a veffel in diftrefs, he perifhed.

The father dying, a tomb is fuppofed to be erected to his memory in the church yard mentioned in Sonnet the 44th. And while a tempeft is gathering, the unfortunate young woman comes thither ; and courting the fame death as had robbed her of her lover, fhe awaits its violence, and is at length overwhelmed by the waves.

G

(82)

VERSE 8. LINE 4.

" And fruitlefs calls on him who cannot hear."

" I fruitlefs mourn to him who cannot hear,
" And weep the more becaufe I weep in vain."

Gray's exquifite Sonnet;
in reading which it is impoffible not to regret
that he wrote only one.

THE ORIGIN OF FLATTERY.

This little poem was written almoft extempore
on occafion of a converfation where many pleafant
things were faid on the fubject of flattery ; and
fome French gentlemen who were of the party,
enquired for a fynonime in Englifh to the French
word fleurette. The poem was inferted in the
two firft editions, and having been afked for by
very refpectable fubfcribers to the prefent, it is re-
printed. The fonnets have been thought too
gloomy ; and the author has been advifed to infert
fome

fome of a more chearful caft.   This poem may by
others be thought too gay, and is indeed fo little
in unifon with the prefent fentiments and feelings
of its author, that it had been wholly omitted but
for the refpectable approbation of thofe to whofe
judgment fhe owed implicit deference.